Sheep and Goat

sheep AND goat

Marleen Westera

ILLUSTRATIONS BY
Sylvia van Ommen

TRANSLATION BY
Nancy Forest-Flier

FRONT STREET 8 LEMNISCAAT
Asheville, North Carolina

Text copyright © 2004 by Marleen Westera
Illustrations copyright © 2004 by Sylvia van Ommen
Originally published under the title *Schaap en Geit* by
Lemniscaat b.v. Rotterdam, 2004

Printed in China
Designed by Helen Robinson
First U.S. edition

Publication has been made possible with financial
support from the Foundation for the Production
and Translation of Dutch Literature.

Westera, Marleen.
[Schaap en Geit. English]
Sheep and goat / by Marleen Westera; illustrations by Sylvia van Ommen;
translated by Nancy Forest-Flier.—1st U.S. ed.
p. cm.
Summary: Follows the daily activities of Sheep and Goat
who, despite often being grouchy or grumpy, are always
there for one another when it counts.
ISBN-13: 978-1-932425-81-9 (hardcover: alk. paper)
[1. Friendship—Fiction. 2. Sheep—Fiction.
3. Goats—Fiction.] I. Ommen, Sylvia van, ill.
II. Forest-Flier, Nancy. III. Title.
PZ7.W519648She 2006
[Fic]—dc22
2006000793

FRONT STREET
An Imprint of Boyds Mills Press, Inc.
A Highlights Company

815 Church Street
Honesdale, Pennsylvania 18431

For Kirsten, who gave me Betje, the sheep

Contents

Quarrel

Sheep and Goat are quarreling. They've been quarreling for three days now.

"You're always in my way," grumbles Sheep.

"You take the tastiest grass," grouches Goat.

And on and on.

It's not much fun in the meadow.

"We can't keep quarreling like this," says Sheep with a sigh. "One of us has to give in."

Goat looks at Sheep. But Sheep won't budge an inch.

"I'll go, then," says Goat.

Sheep says nothing.

Goat strolls over to the fence. She scrambles halfway up to where there's a loose board. Goat pushes the board aside.

She wriggles through the opening and jumps to the ground.

"So long," says Sheep.

Goat opens her mouth, but no sound comes from her throat.

Goat walks along the fence. She looks through.

Sheep is eating. She doesn't even look up.

Goat wants to walk faster. Her legs are moving all right, but they feel funny today—sort of wooden.

Goat has come to the end of the little meadow.

She sees the woods in the distance and starts walking toward them.

It's still very far. Goat takes one step and then another.

She's getting there, but she has a long way to go.

Sheep is concentrating on her food. She gobbles and swallows.

Then Sheep takes a slow look around. She sees Goat near the cornfield. Goat looks very small. Much smaller than usual.

Where is Goat going?

Is she going far, far away?

And will she ever come back again?

When?

Later? Or not until winter?

Sheep takes another nibble of grass. It doesn't taste very good. She's not hungry anymore.

Sheep stares at the cornfield.

Suddenly she sees the farmer. He's sitting on his tractor and driving through the cornfield, on the path where Goat is walking.

But ... Goat has disappeared!

She is nowhere to be seen.

Sheep starts bleating right away, in the direction of the farmer. She bleats very loud. But the farmer doesn't look up.

Sheep runs to the fence.

"Baaaaah!" cries Sheep, as loud as she can.

She stands with her front hooves against the fence. She looks at the farmer. He turns his tractor and drives to the edge of the woods.

Sheep sees something walking there.

Something small and brown.

Goat's legs are tired.

Her mouth is as dry as a bone.

The sun is beating down on her fur.

What Goat really wants to do is lie down. But she has to keep on walking. And walking. And walking.

Suddenly Goat feels two hands. Whoops—she is being picked up. She glides through the air.

Then she's sitting on the tractor, on the farmer's lap.

They ride to the meadow. There's Sheep, waiting for her with a tender tuft of grass in her mouth.

Here they come. The farmer carries Goat firmly under his arm. He lifts her over the fence. Then he drives away.

Goat is back again, standing with Sheep in the meadow.

Sheep doesn't say a word. She keeps chewing her grass.

"That was really fun," squeaks Goat with a hoarse voice. "I saw lots and lots. That's more than you can say, Sheep. You've never been out of the meadow."

"And I never have to be," says Sheep. "The grass here is just fine."

She takes another juicy bite.

Goat turns around.

Her stomach is growling loudly.

She eats a few mouthfuls.

Sheep turns around, too, and sticks her nose in the grass.

They keep on grazing, Goat and Sheep. Back to back.

Family

Goat can tell right away that Sheep is grouchy.

"What's the matter?" asks Goat.

"Nothing," mutters Sheep.

"Fine. Then forget it," says Goat.

Sheep tears off a few blades of grass. She munches slowly and gazes into the distance.

Goat takes a hop and a skip. She bites into a dandelion.

"I miss my family," Sheep blurts out suddenly with a hoarse voice. "They're so far away. And they're all together. I'm here all alone."

"But you've got me," says Goat, chewing on a big tuft of grass.

"That's different," says Sheep. "You're not my family."

"No," says Goat, "I'm Goat."

Sheep stares into the distance. She forgets all about grazing.

Goat grazes for both of them. She doesn't know what to say.

Sheep walks to a corner of the meadow.

She looks at the clouds.

She makes little noises. ...

Sheep is talking. Just talking, to nobody.

Goat sneaks up closer.

"Dear Family," murmurs Sheep with her head in the wind. "How are you? I'm doing pretty well. I live here with Goat. It's all right, but it could be better."

Suddenly Goat has to gulp.

Sheep is quiet for a minute. Then she raises her head again and keeps whispering. "I miss you sometimes. Like today. But most of the time I don't. Not really."

Sheep sticks her nose in the grass and starts eating hungrily.

Goat quickly jumps aside, away from Sheep.

She's not hungry anymore.

She saunters around a bit. But she stays out of Sheep's way.

The afternoon passes slowly.

The sun is still hot.

Suddenly Goat feels something wet against her legs.

She looks down. Sitting there at her feet is Frog.

"Have you seen Sheep?" asks Frog.

"Sheep is over there." Goat points. "At the edge of the meadow."

Frog jumps away, toward Sheep. In a few jumps he's right next to her.

Sheep looks up with surprise.

Frog starts to croak at Sheep.

Goat strains her ears. She quickly moves closer to Sheep and starts chewing.

"Your family lives on the other side of the ditch," croaks

Frog. "They've got one meadow for the eight of them. Their grass is dry and trampled down."

Sheep listens attentively to Frog.

"They're pretty happy. But I hear them complain a lot, too. They complain about how boring it is, with no one but sheep in the meadow. They'd really like a goat, they say."

"A goat?" asks Sheep with surprise.

"Yes. But their farmer doesn't want a goat. They miss you sometimes, too, Sheep. But most of the time they forget to miss you."

Frog gives Sheep a long, hard look.

"They forget a whole lot. Well, so long, Sheep."

With two jumps Frog disappears between the tall blades of grass behind the fence.

Sheep doesn't move. She's stunned.

Goat comes and stands right in front of her.

"What did he say?" asks Goat.

"My family forgets to miss me," says Sheep, her teeth clenched. "They want a goat."

Sheep takes an enormous mouthful of grass.

"They want a goat?" asks Goat with a gleam in her eye. "And are they getting a goat?"

"No. They're not getting a goat."

"Oh, well ...," Goat says, sighing. "Not many sheep can be that lucky."

The Shed

It's a sunny day.

Goat wakes up. She takes a good stretch.

The sun is shining hot on her fur.

Summer! How wonderful!

Goat looks up. The sky is a beautiful blue.

This is something Sheep has got to see ...

Goat runs across the meadow to Sheep's side.

Sheep is still asleep. She is all curled up in the farthest corner of the meadow.

"Sheep! Wake up!" cries Goat. "It's a glorious day! The sun is shining with all its might! This is no time to sleep. The day's a-wasting!"

Goat nudges Sheep with her head.

But Sheep won't wake up.

Sheep doesn't even move.

"It's summer!" cries Goat.

She taps her hoof on Sheep's soft back.

"Sheep, open your eyes!"

Sheep's eyes slowly open halfway. She looks around grumpily.

"What's all the fuss?" she asks.

"It's a beautiful day," says Goat. "Don't miss it."

"I'm still tired," mutters Sheep.

She pushes her nose back into her fleece and goes back to sleep.

"Then I'll look at the sky all by myself," sighs Goat.

She turns her head again to catch the warm, sunny rays.

Goat is enjoying the day.

Suddenly she hears a roaring sound. It's coming from the farmyard. It's the farmer, on his tractor. He's coming to the meadow with the trailer. There's something on it. Something big, something wooden.

The tractor stops next to the fence.

The farmer pulls the big thing off the trailer. He drags it into the meadow, almost to the middle.

Goat walks over and stands nearby.

The farmer gets to work with hammers and stakes.

He's making a big racket.

All the noise wakes up Sheep. She watches from a distance.

The farmer pulls the wooden thing upright. He pushes and pulls.

Goat stands right next to it. Suddenly she sees what it is.

She races off to tell Sheep. "Sheep! We have a shed!"

"Don't need it," mutters Sheep, turning over.

"For when it rains!" shouts Goat.

"It's not raining," Sheep replies. "It's a glorious day."

Sheep makes her way to the edge of the meadow.

"What nonsense. A shed ...," she grumbles.

Goat runs back to the shed.

It's finished and ready.

The farmer picks up his tools and walks out of the meadow.

Goat takes a jump. Then she runs into the shed.

"We have a house," Goat says to herself. "I can hardly believe it."

Goat turns around slowly.

The shed isn't big, but it's very cozy. There's a window in it, too. Goat looks through the window.

She sees Sheep grazing. Sheep is eating today's tastiest grass.

But Goat doesn't care. She stays in the shed. It's so snug. Sheep will come in soon enough.

Goat finds a corner to sit in. Soon she falls asleep.

When Goat wakes up, she sees that Sheep still hasn't come in.

Goat walks over to the doorway. She looks out onto the meadow.

Sheep looks up at the same time. She's standing there chewing her cud.

"Get out of that shack," Sheep bleats with her mouth full. "It's much too nice out here to stay inside. You said so yourself: 'It's a glorious day. Don't miss it. The day's a-wasting.'"

Goat just lets Sheep talk.

She stays in the shed and nibbles on the short grass inside.

Tick, tick, tick. Goat hears something on the roof of the shed.

What's that?

Tock-a-tock-a-tock-a-tock.

Goat sticks her head out.

She feels it right away. Rain.

Goat looks up. The sky is gray. Very dark gray. A big storm coming up ...

Goat pulls her head back in.

She nibbles on an acorn. Tough but tasty.

Sheep comes running. She comes right up to the shed.

She stops at the doorway, right at Goat's feet.

"Move over," she snaps.

"Why?" asks Goat. "You said you didn't need a shed."

Goat doesn't move. Not even a little bit. So Sheep can't get in.

Sheep is getting soaked to the skin. Water is dripping down her legs.

"You thought a shed was nonsense," says Goat with her nose in the air.

"Well," says Sheep. "Sometimes a shed does come in handy. Even I know that. Come on, Goat. Let me in."

"So I was right," says Goat. "I was right, Sheep. Because I said: 'A shed, for when it rains.'"

"Move over, will you?" mutters Sheep.

"Wasn't I right, Sheep?" asks Goat with her head to one side.

Sheep turns around.

She walks to the tree. She stands under the branches.

But it rains right through.

Sheep is getting very wet indeed. Her teeth start chattering.

Goat is comfy and warm, even in front of the doorway.

She looks at Sheep, standing there in the pouring rain.

Sheep's curls have disappeared. Her wool hangs down in limp clumps.

Sheep doesn't look like Sheep anymore.

Goat takes a step back, farther into the shed.

She plucks at the grass. But the grass doesn't taste like anything.

Goat looks out again.

Sheep is still standing under the tree.

Her fleece is completely flat.

That *is* Sheep, isn't it?

Her tail is so thin ...

Goat races out of the shed—*zoom*—and heads for the tree.

She takes a good look at Sheep's head.

It is Sheep, thank goodness.

It's really Sheep.

Goat scrapes the soggy grass with her hoof.

"Sheep," she says in a tiny voice. "You were right. It is nonsense, a shed."

"You think so?" asks Sheep.

"Yes," answers Goat. "We have a tree, haven't we?"

Sick

It's late in the afternoon.

Goat is lying listlessly in the dry grass.

"What's eating you?" asks Sheep.

"I'm sick," says Goat.

"How did you get sick?"

"I don't know."

"What have you got?"

"I don't know."

"Are you going to get better?"

"I don't know that either."

Goat sighs. "You're not asking the right questions, Sheep. You've got to ask different questions. Like, what do I want?" Goat puts her head down. She's too sick to talk very much.

"I don't have to ask you what you want," says Sheep. "Because I know what you want. You want to get better."

"That's true," says Goat. "But I don't know if you can help me get better. You still have to ask me what I want, though, because there's something else I want."

Goat looks wearily at Sheep. She's lying in the grass, thin and motionless.

"Okay," says Sheep. "What do you want, Goat?"

"I want you to come and sit next to me until I fall asleep," peeps Goat.

"Is that all?" asks Sheep with surprise.

"Will you do it?" asks Goat softly.

"Sure," answers Sheep.

Sheep sits down next to Goat.

Goat lays her head on Sheep's lap and closes her eyes.

She shivers a little.

How boring, thinks Sheep, with her leg wrapped around Goat. I'd much rather bleat a song for her. Or knit her a scarf.

Goat keeps tossing and turning. She still can't sleep.

"Shall I pluck the tastiest grass for you?" asks Sheep.

"That's not the right question," whispers Goat. "You have to ask me if I'm comfortable."

"Are you comfortable?" asks Sheep.

"Yes. I'm comfortable."

It takes a long time for Goat to fall asleep. Sheep is getting stiff from all the sitting.

She looks straight ahead, at the shed, at the fence, and at the trees.

The meadow isn't the same without Goat. The meadow is strangely empty.

The sun is going down.

Goat is breathing more restfully. She has fallen asleep.

Now I can stand up, thinks Sheep, and go eat the tastiest grass.

But Sheep doesn't stand up. She keeps on sitting next to Goat.

Later on, when Goat wakes up, Sheep has to ask the right question.

Slowly darkness falls. And Sheep falls asleep.

She dreams that Goat is getting in her way again.

Just as she always does.

It's a very nice dream.

When Goat wakes up, she feels the warm body of Sheep next to her.

She did it! thinks Goat. She stayed with me.

Now Sheep opens her eyes.

"I hope this is the right question, Goat," says Sheep, "but how are you?"

"That is the right question, Sheep," says Goat. "And I'll tell you how I am. I'm still sick. But I slept well."

Company

"Company's coming," says Goat. "I feel it in my hooves. And special company, too. What do you say to that, Sheep?"

Sheep is grazing. She doesn't even look up. "Whatever," she says, smacking her lips.

"Company is on its way. I can smell it!" says Goat. "It's my sister from town, if my nose isn't playing tricks on me."

Goat runs to the fence. She's on the lookout.

"My sister—how can I put this …?" Goat stares into space. Her eyes are all dreamy. "My sister is cleverer than other goats. Cleverer than I am, at any rate."

"Cleverer?" asks Sheep.

"She can do more than other goats," says Goat. "There's something distinguished about her. She's interesting. Not ordinary, like me. She's a petting-zoo goat in the big city! That's nothing to sneeze at, in my opinion."

"Mmm," mutters Sheep. "And what is she going to do here?"

"Just visit," answers Sheep. "Make sure I'm all right. I'm not a successful goat like she is, of course. But it'll be nice for her to see that I'm doing pretty well, too, as a goat."

"Yeah, yeah," mumbles Sheep.

.

"Here she comes!" cries Goat.

Goat points to the road that runs past the farm. And sure enough, there's a goat walking toward them.

"It's her!" cries Goat.

She waves to her sister, who is walking a little stiffly.

She doesn't wave back.

Goat stands with her front hooves against the fence.

"Baaaaaah!" she calls.

But her sister doesn't answer. She walks rather slowly. It takes a very long time before she comes into the meadow.

Goat is at the fence, squirming with impatience.

Finally her sister arrives.

"Come on in," says Goat, and she pushes aside the loose board in the fence. Her sister has to be able to get through the opening.

Sister pushes herself through. Her belly is a little big, but she manages.

"What a terribly narrow passageway," she says.

"That's all we've got," says Sheep.

"And who are you?" asks Sister, glaring at Sheep.

"Sheep!" shouts Goat with enthusiasm. "This is Sheep. What do you think of our meadow, Sister? Isn't it cozy?"

"Well, you could have done worse, I suppose," says Sister.

"Would you like something to eat? A clump of grass? A tuft of hay?"

"I'll have a wheat cake," says Sister with her nose in the air.

"A wheat cake?"

"Two would be nice."

"But we don't have any."

"Oh," says Sister. She gives Goat a cold stare.

"I can see if we still have any dandelions."

"No," says Sister. "Never mind."

"Come on. I'll show you the shed!" cries Goat.

She runs up to the shed.

Sister walks slowly behind her.

"It's still brand-new," says Goat proudly.

"Is this all?" asks Sister. "And where's the straw? Surely it's much too cold here without straw?"

"Sheep and I always stand right next to each other when we're cold."

"You don't seem to have any choice," says Sister. "What a tiny shack."

"Well, it's only for the two of us," says Goat, a bit embarrassed.

She looks over at Sheep, who's rummaging around the shed.

"But how are you doing, Sister?"

Sister straightens her neck.

"*Ex*-cellent. Couldn't be better. Loads of friends at the petting zoo, of course. Wheat cake every day. An e-*nor*-mous climbing board, for all of us. A gigantic stable with mountains of straw. There's never any sheep manure in *our* meadow. The sheep are two meadows away, fortunately."

Sister sticks her nose even higher in the air.

"But I have to leave. I have trouble with all the sheep wool whirling around here. It's getting into my lungs."

She gives a little cough.

She walks out of the shed.

"Come back next year?" asks Goat hopefully.

"We'll see," says Sister.

She wriggles back through the fence.

"Good day," she says thinly.

Sister leaves, walking down the road with a slow, stiff pace.

Goat throws her a kiss. "Until next year!"

Sister doesn't look back.

"And what do you think of her, Sheep?" asks Goat. She looks at Sheep full of expectation.

Sheep looks up midchew.

"I like you more."

Sheep swallows her bit of grass.

"Not that you're so wonderful. But you're better than she is, at any rate."

Goat's mouth falls open. "But she's so—"

"A tuft of hay?" asks Sheep. She shoves a clump of hay toward Goat with her hoof.

"Thank you," says Goat. She peers down the road where Sister was just walking.

She forgets to eat her hay.

"Don't you want your hay?" asks Sheep. "You'd prefer a wheat cake, perhaps?"

Goat looks at Sheep.

Finally she takes a bite of hay.

"No," says Goat. "I prefer hay. How about you?"

"I prefer hay, too," answers Sheep.

It's quiet in the meadow now.

Except for the sound of satisfied munching.

Birthday

"Only three more nights ...," says Goat one morning.

Sheep looks up from her grass with an annoyed look.

"Three more nights, and then what?"

"Three more nights, and then it's my birthday," says Goat. "I can't wait."

Sheep goes back to grazing.

Goat comes up to her. She stands right in front of Sheep.

"What is it?" asks Sheep.

Goat bends over and whispers into Sheep's ear, "You're the only one who's invited."

Sheep looks up with surprise. "Only me?"

"Only you."

"What an honor," says Sheep, beaming.

"You've got to be on time," says Goat. "Otherwise the cake will be gone."

"Fine," says Sheep. "And what do you want for your birthday?"

"I hoped you would ask me that, Sheep. Because I've already decided what I want. I want a compliment."

"A compliment?"

"Yes. It doesn't have to be too long. As long as it's a compliment. So three more nights. Under the tree. At sunrise."

Goat wanders away. She is searching for clover—to put in the cake.

Sheep is thinking. She's thinking hard.

A compliment ...

Where do you get such a thing?

From the wind?

From the bushes?

Maybe from out of the night sky?

Sheep has no idea.

It's a strange sort of present anyway. Just like Goat to ask for something strange.

Why doesn't she ask for hay, or a bed of straw?

Or a piece of tree bark to butt her head against?

Sheep keeps on thinking. For three days.

On the morning of the party she has her present.

All wrapped up and ready.

She knocks on the tree.

Goat welcomes her.

The cake is ready. Grass cake with clover and dandelion leaves.

They both eat. Two pieces each.

"Where's my present?" asks Goat impatiently. "I don't think you've got one with you, Sheep."

Sheep gazes at Goat intently.

"I do too have one, Goat. It's all wrapped up. I'll bring it out later."

Sheep wipes the bits of cake from her snout.

"Goat, I looked everywhere for a compliment. But I couldn't find even one.

"Not in the wind.

"Not in the bushes.

"Not in the night.

"Not even in the quietness.

"I was disappointed. Because I really wanted to give you a compliment.

"When I was as disappointed as I could be, I bumped right into one.

"It's perfect for you.

"It's in my heart.

"I'll unwrap it for you myself.

"Here it comes."

Sheep stands on the big stone under the tree.

She clears her throat.

She looks Goat in the eyes.

She says, with a solemn gesture, "Goat, you are nice."

Sheep doesn't say it very loud. But it sounds so beautiful.

It almost gives Goat goose bumps.

What a wonderful present!

Sheep steps down from the stone.

"Thank you for the party."

"Thank you for coming," whispers Goat.

Sheep walks out from under the tree.

Goat cleans up the mess.

She feels happy.

This was the best birthday Goat has ever had.

The Sparrow

Sheep and Goat are dozing under the tree.

It's their afternoon naptime.

The sun is high in the sky.

It's sweltering.

Everything is still.

The animals.

The people.

The wind.

Sometimes a bee zooms by. But that's all.

Sheep turns over.

She moves a bit farther into the shadows, but it doesn't really help much in this heat.

She lays her head on her hooves.

Her eyes close.

Zzzap!

Sheep sits up with a start. Goat is wide awake, too.

"What was that?" asks Goat.

"Beats me," answers Sheep. "It came from the tree."

"That's impossible," says Goat.

She walks up to the tree.

Suddenly she stops.

She sees something lying on the ground. It's brown, and it's very still.

"Come here, Sheep," squeaks Goat in a tiny voice.

Sheep inches her way toward Goat, with a knot in her stomach.

"The swallow," says Goat quietly. "It's the swallow. He fell. And now he's not moving."

Sheep sees it, too. She gulps. "He flew into the tree. That's what we heard."

"But is he ...?" asks Goat cautiously.

"Yes, he's dead," says Sheep slowly with a nod.

"What do we do now?" asks Goat.

"Be sad," says Sheep. And she looks very upset.

"Yes, we ought to be sad," says Goat. "But not for too long."

"I hardly knew the sparrow," says Sheep. "But the world is different now that he's gone. I'm sure of it."

"Yes, but it's not really that different," says Goat.

"You don't know that," says Sheep. "That remains to be seen."

Goat and Sheep walk back in the heat to where they were dozing.

They lie down again. And keep on sleeping.

When the sun goes down a bit, Sheep and Goat wake up.

"Something happened," says Goat. And she stares into the sky.

"The sparrow is dead," says Sheep.

Goat walks to the tree.

Maybe it was a dream. Or maybe he already flew away.

But the sparrow is really lying there. Right next to the tree.

"It's true, then," says Goat mournfully. "Now I'll never see him flying by again. And I used to love the way he whooshed right over my head."

"You can still keep loving it, can't you?" says Sheep. "Come on. Let's cover him up."

Sheep walks over to the sparrow.

She gently pushes him into a little hole next to one of the tree roots.

She and Goat take some hay from their feeding trough and lay it over the sparrow.

"We'll have to do with one less mouthful," says Goat.

The sparrow is all covered up.

Sheep swallows hard.

"I think the world is really different now," she says hoarsely.

Goat walks back to the feeding trough.

"Not too bad. We've still got hay, just as we always did. Only now we've got a little less."

Goat calmly starts to eat.

Sheep looks up, into the sky.

"There's an empty place here now," she says. "I can feel it."

Goat looks over at Sheep.

"You're exaggerating, Sheep. The meadow is no emptier than it used to be."

Sheep keeps staring up.

"Just imagine, Goat, that *I* was gone for good. Would you just walk back to the feeding trough? And would you say, 'Not too bad. I've still got hay. Even more than I did before'? And would you calmly start eating, just as you're doing now?"

Sheep pushes her front hoof into the ground a bit.

"Come on, Goat. Answer me!"

"I don't know," says Goat. "That remains to be seen."

Pink

Sheep is puffing and panting.

It's a hot summer.

The sun just keeps on shining. Almost every day.

"I'm ready for fall," says Sheep a bit sluggishly.

"Come on! Summer is wonderful," cries Goat.

"You don't have very much fur. That's why you can stand it," says Sheep. "If you had a coat like mine, you'd be singing a different tune."

Suddenly the fence starts to squeak. It's the farmer.

What's he here for?

Goat looks with curiosity.

Sheep doesn't even look up. She's too hot.

The farmer walks up to Sheep.

He has something in his hand. Goat can't see what it is.

He grabs Sheep by the neck.

Sheep looks at the farmer suspiciously.

What's he up to?

He pushes Sheep to the ground!

She's lying on her back. Her legs are thrashing around in the air.

Goat doesn't think much of this at all. She walks up to the

farmer and bumps her head against his legs. But the farmer pushes her away.

"Leave him alone," says Sheep. She's laughing a little. "Just watch, Goat! Watch and see what happens next."

Goat takes a step backward.

She keeps her eye on the farmer. And she keeps her eye firmly on Sheep.

The farmer pushes the thing in his hand onto Sheep's belly. Suddenly the thing starts making a noise. *Zzzzzzzzzzzzzzzzzzzz!*

Sheep doesn't even look scared. In fact, she looks happy.

The farmer runs the thing back and forth across Sheep's belly.

Suddenly Sheep looks sort of pink. ...

Pinker and pinker.

Aha! Sheep is being shorn.

Sheep is really enjoying this.

The shearing goes quickly. There's a whole pile of wool on the grass.

Sheep rolls on her side. She feels wonderful!

"Me, too!" bleats Goat.

"No point shearing you," says Sheep with a loud baah, over the *zzzzzzzzzzzzzzzzzzz*. "Nothing can be made from your fur. But my wool is good for lots of things. Sweaters. Blankets. And socks. All useful things. I'm a useful animal."

"Maybe I'm not useful," says Goat. "But I'm really hot. So I should be shorn."

"Nonsense. You can never be as hot as I was," says Sheep.

The *zzzzzzzzzzzz* stops.

The farmer picks up the pile of wool and walks out of the meadow.

Sheep stands up.

She's completely bald.

She looks very strange. Skinny, and much too naked.

Goat giggles into her hoof.

Sheep feels terrific.

"Oh, that wind on my skin!" she shouts with delight.

"There's hardly any wind at all," Goat grumbles.

"You can't feel it with that thick fur of yours," answers Sheep.

Goat turns around.

Let Sheep bleat, she thinks.

She may feel nice and cool, but she doesn't know how weird she looks.

Extremely weird.

And extremely pink.

Falling

It's a muggy afternoon.

Goat is standing on the big stones under the tree.

She's looking at the leaves hanging over her head.

They look very tasty.

But Goat can't reach them. They're hanging too high.

Goat stretches out her neck. She snaps at the air.

A bleating sound is coming from a corner of the meadow.

It's Sheep. She's watching as Goat snaps at the leaves.

"Forget it," says Sheep. "You'll never reach them."

"Give me a boost, then," shouts Goat.

"Why?" asks Sheep. "Eating grass is enough. You don't have to eat leaves, too."

"Yes, I do," answers Goat. "I *have* to pull a few leaves from a tree every now and then."

"Maybe you're right," says Sheep. "But you're taking your life in your hands. Those stones are slippery."

"Slippery or not, I want leaves," says Goat.

She climbs a bit higher on the stones and reaches up to the leaves once more.

She still can't get to them.

Sheep shakes her head.

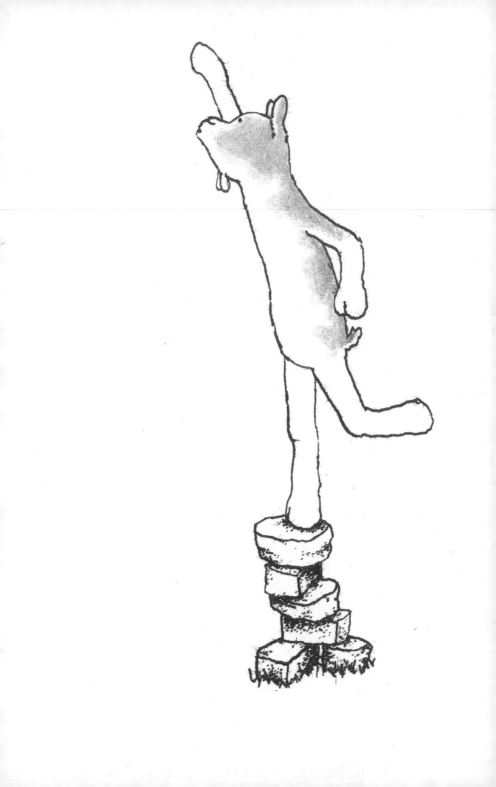

Goat scrambles even higher.

"I've warned you!" shouts Sheep.

Tap! Tap! Goat sets her front hooves against the trunk of the tree. Now she's standing straight up. Her head is sticking between the branches.

Munch! She has grabbed a whole cluster of leaves.

They taste delicious. Goat smacks her lips.

She takes another bite at the leaves. She tears them from the branch.

"Delectable!" she calls to Sheep.

Sheep looks at her crossly. She doesn't say a word.

Just one more bunch, Goat says to herself.

She stretches her neck toward the juicy leaves.

She curls her tongue around them. But just then something starts to slide.

Whoosh! Goat's rear hooves slip back across the stones.

Goat tumbles head over heels. The meadow is spinning before her eyes.

Whap!

Now Goat is lying on the ground. Straight out, right on her belly. Everything hurts, even her tail. The leaves she had pulled at are nowhere to be seen.

Goat looks up unhappily.

"I told you so," says Sheep, chewing languidly on a blade of grass.

Goat carefully pulls herself up on her aching legs.

"You should have listened to me," bleats Sheep. "If you had, that wouldn't have happened."

"But I *have* to tear off a few leaves every now and then," shouts Goat.

"Why?" asks Sheep. "*I* don't have to do any such thing, do I?"

"Well, I do," mutters Goat.

She gives herself a good shake and climbs back up on the stones.

Very quickly this time.

She throws her front hooves against the trunk of the tree.

And she bites into another cluster of leaves.

Sheep sighs.

She can't bear to watch.

Goat lifts her back hooves from the stones.

She scrambles onto a branch. She's quite nimble.

She pulls herself up into the tree.

There she sits. A little wobbly, but she's there, all right. She's sitting in the tree.

Right in front of her nose is a whole row of leaves.

Goat eats them all up.

"Sheep, you want some, too?" shouts Goat. "There's plenty to go around!"

Sheep turns around and walks into the shed.

Goat climbs a little higher.

She really likes the taste of the leaves.

She moves another front hoof.

Shooop! She skids along the bark.

She lands on the ground.

Sheep's head pops out of the shed.

"Your own fault!" she bleats loudly.

"You're right, Sheep." Goat grins with her nose flat in the grass. "It *is* my own fault."

Goat scrambles back up and starts climbing once more.

"And if I fall again, Sheep, it's my fault, too. You don't have to tell me anymore. I already know. It's my own fault."

Sheep listens wearily. She tugs on a clover blossom.

A branch cracks under Goat's rear hooves.

Crunch! Goat is lying in the grass again.

And it's entirely her own fault. Entirely.

Swimming

Summer is almost over.

It's still nice and warm in the meadow.

Goat is skipping all around.

Sheep is trudging back and forth.

"*Quaaaack.*" There's a squawk right near the fence.

Goat sees it first. It's Duck.

She runs over to the fence.

"It's late in the summer. We have a date," squawks Duck.

"A date?" asks Goat.

"Yes, a date. A date to go swimming, to be exact. At the end of the summer, when the ditch isn't cold anymore, you two were going to go swimming with me," says Duck.

"And that's now?" bleats Goat.

"That's now," answers Duck.

Sheep comes shuffling up.

"I don't know anything about any date," she snaps.

"Neither do I," says Goat. "But I'm going."

She's already climbing up the fence.

Sheep doesn't budge.

"Come on. Step on it!" shouts Duck.

Goat jumps to the other side of the fence. She looks back at Sheep from the path.

"Come on," she says.

"Okay, let's go," says Sheep grumpily.

Goat pushes aside the loose board in the fence. Sheep wriggles through. She looks grouchy.

Duck sets out, heading for the ditch.

Goat is jumping all over the place. "How could I have forgotten? What fun. I bet it's really refreshing."

"I'm still not convinced," mutters Sheep.

They're at the ditch.

"Just do what I do," says Duck. "Glide into the water. The rest is automatic. Just keep moving."

Duck walks into the ditch and starts floating.

"Go ahead!" shouts Duck.

Sheep is sitting in the grass at the edge of the ditch.

"I think I'll just dip my hooves," she says.

She slides her back hooves into the water.

"That doesn't count!" shouts Goat. "That's not swimming. It doesn't even look like swimming. I'm going to really go swimming. Watch me, Sheep! Here I go!"

Goat takes a running jump.

Splash! She bounds into the ditch. The water flies up high. Goat starts making strange sounds. She's doesn't swim nearly as gracefully as Duck.

Sheep watches her anxiously.

Goat moves all her legs at once, but she doesn't stay afloat. She sinks into the dark water.

Duck has already reached the bridge. He doesn't even turn around.

"Wait for meeeeee!" cries Goat feebly down the ditch.

She comes up for just a minute. Then right away she sinks back down. Sheep can see only her tail. And some splashing and bubbles.

Sheep quickly pulls her rear hooves out of the water.

She walks to the first bush she sees and tears off a long branch with her teeth.

"This way!" calls Duck in the distance.

"Wait for meeeeee!" wails Goat.

"I'm coming!" shouts Sheep.

She runs to the edge of the ditch with the branch in her mouth. Sheep swings one end of the branch into the ditch, right near Goat. She holds the far end firmly between her teeth.

"Grub hld wth yr teth!" shouts Sheep. "Grub hld wth yr teth, Goat. I'll pll you in frm ths sid."

Goat splashes wildly all around the branch. Her head keeps coming up. She tries to grab the branch with her teeth. But she misses.

"Agin!" shouts Sheep.

Goat tries again and misses.

She sputters and blubbers.

Sheep starts sweating.

Duck comes back. He's taking his time. He swims right up to Goat.

"That's pathetic," he quacks.

"Wu hv to sv hr!" screams Sheep. "Psh the brnch un hr muth!"

"Blurggg," says Goat.

"Whatever you say," says Duck.

He grabs the branch in his beak. And with one firm swing he sweeps it into Goat's mouth.

"Gtcha," squeaks Goat, coughing.

Sheep starts to pull with all her might.

Goat stops splashing and lets herself be hauled in through the water.

Sheep heaves as hard as she can.

Just a little bit farther ...

Goat gets to the edge of the ditch. She lets go of the branch.

Sheep reaches out a hoof.

"I'll climb out myself," says Goat.

Goat steps onto the bank.

And stands there. Dripping wet.

Sheep spits out the branch. She looks Goat straight in the eyes.

"That was a close call."

Goat doesn't say anything. She is shivering all over. She just looks at the ground.

Duck comes waddling up.

"I had imagined something quite different for this afternoon," he says.

"Me, too," says Goat. "You went much too fast, Duck. I couldn't keep up. I'm much heavier than you are. It's harder for me to swim. But I did pretty well, don't you think?"

Duck keeps his beak shut.

"Let's go," says Sheep. "So long, Duck."

"Adieu," says Duck.

And he plunges back into the water.

•

"Ah-choo!" sneezes Goat. Water comes flying out of her nose.

Sheep has already started walking. Goat comes running up behind her.

"Even so, I'd like to try swimming again sometime," says Goat.

Sheep turns around. "Oh, yes?"

"Yes," answers Goat. "But not with Duck."

Dreams

The sun has just come up.

The grass is wet with dew.

Sheep is already awake. She's taking a little stroll.

Goat is still asleep, curled up in the shed.

Peace and quiet, muses Sheep. The whole meadow to myself. No one to get in my way. No yammering and complaining. I ought to get up early more often.

Sheep nibbles on the grass. It's very short. Almost too short to eat.

But near the fence Sheep sees some longer blades.

She walks over. She takes a few bites. Very tasty.

Look at that! Right behind the fence is a whole bunch of dandelions. With lots and lots of leaves around them.

If Sheep were to stick her snout under the fence, she might be able to reach them.

She tries it. No. No luck.

Sheep lies flat on her belly.

She shoves her head farther under the fence. She sticks out her long tongue and tries to reach the dandelions. Bingo! She pulls the flowers off with her tongue.

How juicy they are. Sheep just lies there enjoying herself.

Another mouthful of flowers. These are delicious, too.

And another bunch of leaves.

There are rows and rows.

Sheep eats and eats. All along the fence.

Goat is still nowhere to be seen.

Sheep keeps on eating. But suddenly she stops.

This isn't right, she thinks. I ought to save something for Goat.

Sheep jumps up.

She walks to the shed. It's still quiet inside.

Goat is lying on one ear.

Sheep starts bleating. Very loud and very long.

Goat wakes up with a start. She looks around with a befuddled look in her eyes. But she also seems very, very happy.

"I've just discovered lots and lots of dandelions," says Sheep.

"Oh," says Goat.

"There," says Sheep, pointing. "Want to come with me?"

"No," says Goat.

"No?"

"No. I have to finish my dream."

"Finish your dream? It's too late for that. You're awake now."

"But I'm going back to sleep. I have to find out how my dream ends, don't I?" says Goat firmly.

"What were you dreaming about?" asks Sheep.

"About goats. And mountains.

"And rocks and slopes.

"We were climbing. We got to the top. Some didn't make it. But I got very far.

"Maybe I'll be the first to get to the top.

"So long, Sheep."

Goat puts her head back on her hooves. She closes her eyes tight.

Sheep looks at her with surprise.

What's going on? Goat not jumping at the chance to eat some tender dandelions ...

Strange.

"Goat?" says Sheep. "I'm afraid I'll end up eating all the dandelions myself if you don't come with me."

Goat starts out of her sleep once again. "What did you say, Sheep?"

"I'm going to eat all the dandelions myself."

"Enjoy them, Sheep."

"And the leaves, too."

"Good night," says Goat. "I'm on my way to the top. I'm almost there."

Goat starts dozing once more.

"Suit yourself," mutters Sheep.

She turns around. And she walks back to the fence.

She throws herself on her belly and squeezes her head underneath.

She eats an outrageous amount of dandelions. And

even more leaves. She keeps eating until she can hardly eat anymore.

Just as she's scrambling to her feet Sheep hears Goat behind her.

"I made it," says Goat proudly.

Sheep quickly swallows her last bite.

"What did you make?"

"I got to the top. I was the first, Sheep. The first."

"Oh, that dream of yours." Sheep sighs.

"The whole goat colony cheered for me," says Goat with a gleam in her eyes.

"Goat, it was just a dream. There was so much that you missed. Lots of dandelions. With leaves."

"Not important," says Goat. "I'll just have to go hungry today. But they cheered for me. The whole herd. From the rocky cliffs. They thought I was fantastic. And I am, too."

Goat looks satisfied.

Sheep is dragging herself around in a little circle.

"My stomach is rather full," she puffs. "I think I'll go take a nap.

"Maybe I'll dream of something nice. Like a flock of sheep perhaps.

"A big flock of sheep ...

"And a shepherd who counts us all.

"But he doesn't count me. Because I'm missing.

"So he starts searching for me.

"And when he finds me, he's *so* happy."

Sheep stares with a dreamy look in her eyes.

"He takes me on his lap. And he gives me a dandelion.

"But I'd rather have heather.

"He has heather, too.

"Help me look!" shouts Sheep.

"No, I'm much too comfortable here," says Goat, smacking her lips.

"Come on! You've got to have some energy left for a little happiness."

"I wonder if that's true," answers Goat.

She keeps on chewing with a look of satisfaction on her face.

"Then I'll look all by myself. But if I find happiness, I'm going to keep it," says Sheep.

"Good luck!" calls Goat.

Suddenly Sheep runs to the fence.

She pushes herself through the opening. She looks very determined.

And so strange.

For a while it's very noisy. Then suddenly it's very quiet. Sheep has never heard these sounds before, or this silence.

The air is getting colder and colder.

Sheep shivers a little.

Is happiness somewhere around here? Probably not, thinks Sheep.

She stands still. She looks all around.

Happiness must be on the other side of the meadow.

Sheep turns around. She starts walking again.

She walks in the opposite direction. Back past the tractors, the stables, the house, and the cows.

She's already back at her own meadow.

Goat starts jumping around. She sees Sheep walking up. "Have you come back?" she asks hopefully.

"Of course not," says Sheep.

"Did you find happiness?"

"Not yet. But now I know which way I have to go. That way."

Sheep points with her front hoof.

She walks farther.

Goat gulps.

She waves to Sheep. But Sheep doesn't notice.

Sheep walks past the shed. Past bushes and trees. She walks past the chickens, but she doesn't say hello. She's too busy looking. Looking for happiness.

Then Sheep sees a little meadow. With beautiful green grass. Greener than she has ever seen in her life.

The meadow is empty. There's no one in it.

Sheep walks up.

She looks over the fence.

The bright green grass waves gently in the breeze. It looks terribly juicy.

It has to be here.

Where else could it be?

Sheep pushes against the gate. It opens in a snap.

Sheep walks into the meadow.

The grass comes up to her knees.

Sheep sticks her nose between the long blades.

That tickly feeling ... That fragrance!

Sheep knows for sure: This is where happiness is!

Sheep begins eating.

The grass tastes terrific.

She has never tasted such tender grass.

She eats until she's full. Then she lies down.

How soft this grass is!

Sheep falls asleep.

She lies there dozing. For hours.

Sheep wakes up well rested.

She stands right up.

She has made up her mind. She's going to tell Goat that she has found happiness.

So she was right. You have to look for happiness by yourself. It won't come to you.

Sheep walks to the gate. She pushes against it.

But the gate won't open. She'll have to pull it.

Sheep pulls and pulls.

After pulling very hard, she manages to get the gate open a little. But just as she's about to walk through, the gate snaps shut right before her eyes.

And there aren't any loose boards in the fence that she can shove to one side.

She can't get out.

She can't get to Goat.

Sheep takes a few steps through the juicy grass.

If only Goat would come ...

But Goat is back in the meadow waiting for happiness to come to her.

Sheep goes back to eating. But the beautiful green grass doesn't taste nearly as good as it did before.

Darkness is slowly falling.

Suddenly this meadow looks very different.

The wind in the trees is making strange sounds.

Sheep doesn't want to listen. But the more she doesn't want to listen, the more she hears.

Crashing.

Rattling.

Stamping of hooves.

Is it coming from the path?

Sheep turns to the dark path and stares.

It's the farmer, with his horse on a rope.

He's coming to Sheep's meadow.

He throws the gate open. Then he loosens the rope. The horse runs into the meadow.

Not this, too, Sheep says to herself. She quickly dives into a corner.

The horse starts to whinny. He makes wild jumps. Sheep doesn't dare look. How big the horse is!

Sheep makes herself as small as she can.

She lies very still.

Her heart is pounding.

Suddenly Sheep feels something soft and warm on her neck.

Carefully she opens her eyes.

It's the farmer. His hand is on Sheep's neck.

He picks her up and leads her out of the meadow.

The horse is snorting.

The gate closes again.

They walk down the path. The farmer takes big steps. Sheep scampers right beside him.

Finally they arrive at Sheep's own meadow. Goat is standing at the fence.

The farmer lets Sheep in. Then he goes away.

Sheep is standing right up next to Goat.

It's a peaceful evening. And not as dark as it was before.

"Well, did you find happiness?" asks Goat.

"I thought I had. But I was wrong. I'm sorry."

"That's all right, Sheep," says Goat. "Would you like a mouthful of hay? It's a little dry today."

"It doesn't matter," says Sheep. She takes a big bite.

It *is* dry, and a little dusty. But it tastes like happiness.

The Storm

The wind is howling.

The branches of the tree are swishing back and forth.

Leaves are flying all around.

Goat runs to Sheep, who is calmly grazing.

"Sure is windy, isn't it, Sheep?" bleats Goat.

"This isn't just wind," answers Sheep. "This is a storm."

Sheep starts eating again.

The fence rattles.

Goat looks frightened. The sky is in an uproar.

"Sheep, I don't like this," says Goat in a tiny little voice.

"Who does?" mutters Sheep. "Storms are never fun. But it will pass."

The fence rattles again. But much louder than before.

Sheep keeps on chewing. Just the way she always does.

A branch zips past.

A shiver goes down Goat's back.

The storm whooshes past her body with enormous force. She has to lean into it just to stay standing.

It blows harder and harder.

"What should we do?" squeaks Goat anxiously to Sheep.

"We'll go to the shed," says Sheep. "Then we'll be safe."

Sheep walks to the shed. Goat scurries along beside her.
The storm rages. It's hard to walk in such a wind.
But soon they're inside.
Goat huddles next to Sheep.
"Nothing can happen in here," says Sheep reassuringly.
"That's good," whispers Goat.
She pushes her nose into Sheep's wool.

Sheep looks outside and watches everything that's going on.
The sky is very dark.
The storm is still howling.
The fence around the meadow is all twisted.
Sheep's eyes widen.
"What's the matter?" asks Goat.
"Nothing," says Sheep.
"Really nothing?"
"Of course not!" says Sheep bravely. "There's absolutely
nothing wrong."

There they are. Listening. To the noise of the storm.
"When's it going to stop?" asks Goat cautiously.
"It's sure to stop soon. And we're safe in here, aren't we?"
Sheep's voice sounds very calm.
The storm keeps on raging. It pounds against the walls
of the shed.
Something starts to crack. It's a squeaky crack. And it's
very close. It's in the shed.
"The shed's going to collapse!" Goat screams in panic.

"That's impossible," says Sheep. "It's a good sturdy shed."

"But it's also a good sturdy storm," whimpers Goat.

The cracking gets louder.

Sheep stares straight ahead.

The storm roars and whistles.

The shed starts to shake. It's squeaking in every corner.

Goat huddles up against Sheep as close as she can.

Sheep doesn't say a word. She looks around the shed hastily.

The look on her face is different now. Goat sees it.

Sheep takes a step forward until her head sticks out of the shed.

The wind beats around her ears. She quickly takes another step back.

There they are.

Saying nothing.

Then *WHAP!*

And *boink.*

And *rum-tum-tum.*

Something's falling on the roof. And rolling off again.

"I'm scared," bleats Goat.

"Don't be," says Sheep. "We're safe here."

Once again something taps on the roof.

And again.

And again.

"Acorns," says Sheep.

The storm screeches even louder. It hammers away at the shed.

It shrieks in the air.

It makes a deafening racket.

A crash.

A bang.

Moaning and clattering.

Goat can hardly breathe.

Sheep cowers.

"Don't worry," Goat hears her say.

They squeeze their eyes tight shut, both of them.

Once more there's a crashing and a hammering and a cracking. It's very close.

A cold wind comes tearing inside and rushes around the shed.

Goat shivers.

Sheep trembles.

Then it's quiet.

"Sheep?" says Goat softly, with her eyes squeezed shut. "We're still alive, aren't we?"

"Yes. We're still alive, Goat. But something happened. Do you know what it is?"

"No. Shall we look? I'll count to three. Then we'll open our eyes."

Goat counts to three.

They open their eyes.

It's light in the shed. Lighter than usual.

Goat looks up.

She sees light. Clear light.

"The storm is gone, Sheep. *That*'s what happened."

Sheep looks up, too.

All she can see is blue. Sky blue.

"The roof, Goat!" bleats Sheep. "The roof is gone!"

Now Goat sees it as well. She's standing under the open sky. The sun slowly appears.

Goat runs out of the shed. She's looking for the roof. It's right behind the shed. "Sheep! Come see! The roof is still in one piece!"

Sheep comes out of the shed. She taps the roof with her hoof.

"Everything will be fine," she says hoarsely. "The farmer can put it right back on."

They take a walk around the meadow side by side.

Everywhere there are branches and bits of bark that were blown from the tree.

Suddenly Goat stops. She looks at Sheep. "Were you scared, Sheep?"

"How could I be?" replies Sheep. "You were already scared."

"That's true," murmurs Goat. She looks at the ground.

"It doesn't matter," says Sheep. "But, Goat, when the next storm comes, can I be the one who's scared? And you be brave? And you reassure me?"

"All right," answers Goat. "Then I'll say, 'Nothing to worry about, Sheep. Everything's going to be fine.' Does that sound brave?"

Sheep nods with satisfaction.

"Very brave, Goat. Very brave."

They shuffle along, thinking about the next storm.

Sheep can hardly wait.

Longing

Goat wakes up.

She blinks her eyes in the bright sunlight.

Beside her is Sheep, still sleeping.

Goat stretches out her four legs and springs up with a spirited jump.

"Sheep?" asks Goat, rather loudly.

Sheep looks up lazily. She grumbles and mutters. "It's still too early."

"Sheep, do you know what longing is?"

"Yes," answers Sheep. "I know what longing is. But now I'm going back to sleep."

"Sheep! Stay awake, will you!" shouts Goat. "You've got to explain it to me. Longing ... what is that? I've heard of it before. But I don't know what it is."

Goat hops back and forth. "It sounds very beautiful indeed. It must be something beautiful. Longing ... *long-ing* ...," says Goat slowly, with an outstretched neck. "Doesn't that sound beautiful to you, Sheep?"

Sheep squeezes her eyes half shut. "Not at the moment, Goat. I want to sleep."

"But the day has started. It's a good time to talk about longing."

Goat taps Sheep on her shoulder. "Get up, Sheep."

But Sheep doesn't get up. She sighs. "Sometimes," she says slowly, "sometimes I long for a little more peace and quiet."

"Sheep! You're longing!" shouts Goat. She beams from ear to ear. "You're longing! You said so yourself. You're longing for peace and quiet. How does that feel, Sheep? Longing for peace and quiet? I want to know."

Sheep looks a little blurry-eyed. "Yes," she says. "I'm longing for peace and quiet. It feels wonderful and sad at the same time."

Sheep has a strange look in her eyes. "It's wonderful to think about it. About peace and quiet. About lots of peace and quiet. But I don't have peace and quiet, Goat. And I'm not going to get much peace and quiet, not right now. And that's too bad. It's really too bad."

Goat listens intently.

Sheep looks a little sad.

Goat looks at the ground. "So that's what longing is," she says. "You think about something nice. But the nice thing is something you don't have."

"That's right," says Sheep.

"Then I'm longing, too!" says Goat. "I'm longing in the worst way for birch branches. To chew on."

"That's not really longing," says Sheep. "You have plenty of other branches to chew."

"But birch branches are the crunchiest. That's why I'm longing for birch branches."

"Even so, it isn't really longing. I'm longing for peace and quiet. *That's* real. Because I'm not getting any peace and quiet, I can only think about it. And I can only imagine how wonderful it would be to have a little peace and quiet. You nibble all day long on all kinds of branches. So you don't have to long for branches."

Sheep puts her head back down. "There. I'm finished talking about longing. Now let me have some peace and quiet, Goat."

Sheep closes her eyes tight and tries to go back to sleep.

"Don't fall asleep, Sheep!" cries Goat. "I'm longing for you!"

"That's impossible," mutters Sheep. "I'm here already. You can't long for something that's already here."

"But I'm longing to talk to you," says Goat.

"You just have."

"But I'm longing for more, Sheep."

"Go right ahead, Goat. I'd even say that's a good thing," says Sheep. "Look, Goat. I'm going to go to sleep. And you're going to long to talk to me some more."

Sheep looks at Goat closely. "You're going to imagine it. That you're talking to me some more. You really want to talk to me. But you don't know when that's ever going to happen. It's not happening now, at any rate."

"Oh no?" asks Goat.

"No. If I keep talking to you now, you can't long to talk to me. And that would be a shame. Longing is so nice. It's something you've got to enjoy."

Sheep closes her eyes.

She falls asleep right away. Goat sees it. Sheep has all the peace and quiet she wants.

But she can't have it. Sheep has to *long* for peace and quiet. That's much nicer.

Goat charges up to her. "Sheep! Wake up! That's not the way to long for peace and quiet."

Sheep opens her eyes. She stares straight ahead with a grumpy look.

"Sometimes I don't know what's nicer ... longing for something ... or getting what you're longing for."

"Yes!" shouts Goat. "Let's talk about that, Sheep! About what's nicer."

Sheep shakes her head.

She doesn't want to talk.
She wants to nap. To nap forever.
But she doesn't know when that's ever going to happen.

Cow

There's the sound of mooing in the morning mist.

Goat wakes up with a start.

Moooooooooo! The mooing is not far away.

It's coming from the path. Goat can hear it.

She can't see very much, though. The mist is too thick.

Moooooooooo! Now it's right near the fence.

Goat springs to her feet.

She trots along in the direction of the fence.

It's white all around her. White from the mist.

But Goat can see the fence already. She's about to put her front hooves up against it, but suddenly she stops.

A big head is looking at her over the fence.

It's Cow.

The gate swings open.

Goat shrinks back.

Through the thick mist, Goat watches as Cow steps into the meadow.

Very slowly.

The farmer is walking beside her. He's got a rope around Cow's neck. He pulls her farther into the meadow, loosens the rope, and lets her go. Then the farmer walks away.

Cow shakes her head. She looks at Goat drowsily.

"Good morning," says Goat. "Have you moved in here? Or have you come to visit?"

Goat looks at Cow. But Cow doesn't say anything.

"Would you like some buttercups? Freshly picked?" Goat starts looking for buttercups. It's not easy to find them in the mist.

Cow still doesn't say anything.

"Wait a minute! I'll get Sheep," says Goat. "Sheep lives here, too."

"Moooooooooo!" lows Cow, very loudly.

Goat wants to run to Sheep, but she doesn't see her anywhere. The mist is still very low.

Goat looks all around.

"Moooooooooo!" cries Cow again across the misty meadow. It's a peaceful sound.

Suddenly there's Sheep, right in front of Goat's nose.

"What's this all about?"

"Cow has come!" cries Goat through the mist.

"And when is Cow going away?" asks Sheep grumpily.

"Mooooooooooo!" lows Cow.

"But she has just arrived," says Goat.

"That may very well be true. But she has no business here."

Goat looks at Cow. She's staring straight ahead, looking rather forlorn.

"Oooh!" cries Goat. "I promised her some buttercups."

"That's just great!" screams Sheep. "You start right in by giving away our buttercups. She can just eat grass, can't she?"

"Moooooooooo!" says Cow. She sounds a little miserable.

Sheep turns around. She walks quickly to the feeding trough and starts in on the hay.

Goat picks a buttercup.

She takes it to Cow. Cow swallows it.

Goat gets some more. Cow smacks her lips with pleasure.

The mist is rising now.

Goat sees Sheep standing at the feeding trough. The feeding trough is suddenly completely empty.

Sheep gobbles the last stalks of hay.

Goat finds one more buttercup. She shares it with Cow. Then she eats some grass. Cow eats with her.

Cow lies down nearby. She starts chewing her cud.

"May I come chew my cud next to you?" asks Goat.

Cow doesn't say a thing.

So Goat cuddles up next to Cow.

They lie side by side chewing their cud. For hours and hours.

Sheep stays far away. She strolls around the meadow. Her belly is stretched tight.

She walks to the fence. She looks down the path. But no one is coming.

When is Cow going to be taken away?

Will she stay long?

Sheep starts strolling again.

She glares at Goat, who is still lying next to Cow. It's a strange sight.

Then the gate rattles.

It's the farmer. He walks right up to Cow and ties a rope around her neck.

He takes Cow back with him.

Goat runs behind Cow. But Cow has already passed through the gate.

She looks around for a moment.

"Moooooooooo!" she calls to Goat.

The farmer pulls the gate shut.

Goat watches Cow until she's gone around the curve.

"Well." Sheep sighs.

"Cow didn't stay very long," says Goat.

"Long enough," answers Sheep. "And now I'm tired. Terribly tired."

Sheep almost collapses.

"Are you just tired? Or maybe a bit heavy, too?"

Sheep looks at Goat. Her belly is pressed against her legs.

"Lots of cud to chew?" asks Goat.

"Sort of," answers Sheep.

"You can come chew your cud next to me," says Goat.

"Thanks," says Sheep softly.

She walks up to Goat.

"Can I stay for a long time?" asks Sheep. "Hours and hours?"

"Of course," answers Goat.

They lie down. And start chewing. Until deep in the night.

Being Alone

It's a chilly morning.

Sheep is searching for daisies. She can't find any. And Goat keeps getting in the way.

"Goat," begins Sheep, "why don't you go stand over there? You're bothering me."

"I'm bothering you?" asks Goat. "But I'm not doing anything."

"You're in my way. Go find another piece of meadow, Goat. I'll see you later on tonight."

Goat pulls up a daisy. She gives it to Sheep.

"Thanks," says Sheep coldly. "Until tonight, then."

Goat looks at Sheep. And then Goat looks down at the ground.

Slowly she turns around.

Then she walks away, all the way to the back of the meadow.

It's much colder there. And the grass is tough.

Goat walks around a bit with her head down.

The wind cuts right through her fur.

Goat shivers all over.

She steals a glance over at Sheep.

Sheep is eating daisies. Sheep isn't cold.
She's out of the wind, right next to the shed.

Goat knows what this means: Sheep wants to be alone.
She often wants to be alone.
But it's still strange.

Goat spits out a mouthful of grass.
Is it nighttime yet?
"Sheep!" calls Goat across the cool meadow. "Is it night-time yet?"
"Not by a long shot," grumbles Sheep. She doesn't even look up.
"Should I wave to you every now and then?" calls Goat.
"Go ahead," says Sheep. "But I won't wave back."
Goat starts waving.
But Sheep just keeps on grazing.
Goat puts her front hoof down again.
She feels like running, right across the meadow.
Goat shakes her legs to keep warm. Then she runs through the meadow at full speed.
She shoots straight past Sheep and just misses her.
She ends up in the other corner, near the blackberry bush.
Goat fills her lungs with air.
For just a minute she was close to Sheep.

Sheep must have noticed.

She looks up at Goat with a frown.

Goat quickly takes a bite of grass. It feels cold in her mouth.

In this corner of the meadow the wind is really blowing hard.

Goat's fur stands straight up.

Goat wants to be near the shed. It's less windy there.

She walks up to the side of the shed, very quietly.

Sheep can't see her. She's standing just behind the shed now.

Goat is near the shed. She's right next to the wall. She's almost leaning against it.

But the wind keeps blowing very hard. Goat can't stand being out in the cold any longer.

Quickly she slips into the shed.

Here there's no wind. Here Goat feels fine.

And she's right near Sheep. She can see her through the window.

Sheep is still grazing. She has already eaten mountains of daisies. Goat sees there is not a single daisy left.

Now Sheep is looking around.

She looks all over the meadow.

Suddenly she starts to run. She runs to one corner of the meadow, then to another. Sheep races to the feeding trough. She looks in it. And behind it. She walks over to the fence and tries as best she can to look over it. She runs to the tree and stares up into the branches.

Then Sheep starts calling, "Yoo-hoo, Goat! Where are you?"

Goat's heart suddenly starts beating faster.

"Go-oat!" she hears across the windy meadow.

Goat keeps still.

Sheep wanted to be alone, didn't she? It's not even night-time yet. The sky is still light.

"Goat! Answer me! Where are you?"

Sheep's voice trembles a little.

Goat peeks through the window.

Sheep walks up to the shed on wobbly legs. She looks worried.

Suddenly there she is at the doorway. She's looking down at the ground.

She huffs and puffs. She doesn't see Goat standing there.

"Hello," says Goat dryly.

"Oh ... hello," stammers Sheep, looking up with surprise. She turns her eyes away from Goat.

"I wanted to get out of the wind," Sheep bleats awkwardly.

"Me, too," answers Goat. "But I'll leave."

"You don't have to," says Sheep.

"But it's not even nighttime," says Goat.

"Oh, come on," says Sheep. "Just stay here. I know you like to be near me. So I'll make an exception this time."

Sheep looks at Goat with glistening eyes.

It's quiet in the shed.

Outside you can hear the wind.

Sheep snuggles up next to Goat.

"Am I bothering you, Sheep?" asks Goat softly. "Just tell me if I am. Promise?"

"I promise," answers Sheep.

Tummyache

The morning is warm. The meadow is full of life. Bees, dragonflies, beetles, worms ...

Goat is jumping all over the place. She's glad to be awake.

Sheep is awake, too. But she's not doing very much.

She's just standing there. Not walking. Not eating.

She peers around with a dull look on her face.

Taking tiny steps, she shuffles up to Goat.

"Goat," says Sheep, "the dandelions are at their best, I see. They look wonderful. We really ought to eat them all up today."

"Sounds good to me," says Goat.

"But wait a minute," says Sheep. "I've got a terrible tummyache. I can't eat. That's the problem. Yet it's such a shame for the dandelions if we don't eat them up today. They will have grown for nothing."

"Then *you* eat a few tomorrow," says Goat.

"Tomorrow they'll all have gone to seed. They'll be nothing but fluff. And they won't taste like anything."

Sheep looks sadly at the bright yellow dandelions growing between her front hooves.

"All those dandelions have grown for nothing. All those

dandelions that I can't eat. It's such a waste, Goat." Sheep
bows her head.

Goat looks around the meadow.
    It's bursting with dandelions, all in full bloom.
    "I'll eat some for you!" cries Goat. "I'll eat them all. They
won't have grown for nothing. Don't worry, Sheep."
    Sheep turns her ears. She looks at Goat with surprise.
    Goat starts right in. She eats one flower after another.
There are lots and lots. But Goat can easily eat them all.
    Sheep has gone to lie down. She looks on calmly.

She rubs her tummy. It still hurts.

Sheep shuts her eyes for a minute.

The tractor is chugging down the path.

Sheep looks up.

The farmer is driving past the meadow. With a wagon full of vegetables. Carrots, beets, and cabbages.

The tractor is making a terrific noise.

The trailer bounces up and down. Something rolls off. A juicy cabbage.

It looks very nice to Sheep. Green, and very round.

The cabbage rolls down the path. Right up to the fence. And there it stops.

Sheep keeps looking at it.

What a terrible waste.

That cabbage is never going to get eaten if it just lies there on the edge of the path.

That cabbage grew for nothing.

How dreadful.

Sheep stands up.

She ambles over to Goat, who's walking around doing nothing.

"Come on over to the fence," says Sheep.

Goat scampers along with Sheep.

"You see that cabbage there?" says Sheep, pointing with her front hoof.

"I see it," says Goat.

"It fell off the wagon. Now it's lying here. There's no one

to eat it. I think it's such a waste and I still have a tummy-ache."

Sheep looks very dejected.

Goat pushes the board in the fence to one side.

"I'll go get it. And I'll eat it. Otherwise it's just too sad."

Goat creeps through the fence.

She walks up to the cabbage. She clamps it between her teeth and pops it through the fence. Then she steps back into the meadow.

"I'll start right away," says Goat. "Tomorrow it may not be good anymore."

Goat starts nibbling on the cabbage.

Sheep lies down again.

Good. The cabbage is saved.

Goat munches and gnaws. The cabbage is pretty tough. Goat has to chew very hard.

It takes until evening to get it all eaten.

Goat licks her lips clean.

She lies down next to Sheep and rubs her tummy.

"How great," says Sheep softly. "The dandelions didn't bloom so beautifully for nothing ... and the cabbage didn't grow for nothing ... and it's all thanks to you, Goat."

"Yes," says Goat. "All thanks to me."

For a moment they say nothing.

"Sheep," says Goat cautiously. "I believe I have a tummy-ache."

Sheep leans her head on Goat's neck.

"Then tomorrow I'll eat for you, Goat. But now it's time to sleep. The day is over."

The Fence

It's a cloudy morning.

Goat is standing near the fence. She peers through. Raindrops are falling on her neck.

Outside the fence it looks just as gray as it does in the meadow.

Sheep is walking along with her nose in the grass.

Goat steps up to her.

"Say, Sheep," begins Goat, "what do you think of our fence?"

"I don't think anything of our fence," says Sheep.

"What? Nothing at all?" asks Goat.

"No. Nothing at all."

Sheep takes a bite of grass.

"Don't you think our fence is too tall? Or too low? Or too rickety? Or too old? Maybe too sturdy? Or too brown? Or maybe you think the fence shouldn't be there at all?" asks Goat.

"No," answers Sheep, "I don't think any of those things."

Sheep walks to the drinking trough. She takes a big gulp of water.

"But," Goat continues, "don't you ever wonder what our

life would be like if we had a different fence? Or if we didn't have *any* fence around our meadow?"

"No," says Sheep, "I never wonder that. This is our fence. I think it's a fine fence."

"But, Sheep," says Goat, looking up, "if we had a very tall fence that you couldn't look over or through, that wouldn't be very nice."

"But we don't have that," says Sheep.

"Just imagine, though!" shouts Goat. "That we didn't have any fence at all!"

"That's impossible," mutters Sheep. "Every meadow has a fence around it."

"But if we didn't have a fence," muses Goat, "we could just go wherever we liked." Goat looks dreamily over the top of the fence.

"But that's not necessary," mutters Sheep.

Goat jumps. She lands right in front of Sheep.

"But Sheep! Actually ... actually, we don't have a fence. Because we can go through it. The loose board, Sheep! We can go wherever we like!"

"We've already done that. And we didn't enjoy it," says Sheep, annoyed. "Stop this business about the fence. And, anyway, that passageway by the loose board is too tight for me."

"We can make it bigger."

Goat pushes at the loose board with her hoof.

"I'm going to the shed," mumbles Sheep. "It's getting too wet for me."

Sheep lumbers off to the shed.

Goat is still pushing against the board in the fence.

It's a bit looser already.

Goat takes a running jump. She bonks the board with her head.

The board falls off. It's lying on the path.

Now the hole in the fence is very big. It looks odd.

Goat steps through.

She doesn't have any idea where she wants to go.

First she wants to go to the shed. To stand next to Sheep for a while.

Goat walks to the shed. It's dry in there. And there's a heap of straw inside.

Goat and Sheep eat the straw. It's very good straw.

Good to lie down on, too. They take a nap together in the warm straw.

Late in the afternoon Sheep suddenly wakes up.

She hears a banging sound.

Sheep stands right up.

She sticks her head out of the shed.

The farmer is standing at the fence. He's hammering the board back tight. He's even hammering an extra board on.

Now there's no hole anymore.

The farmer is finished. He walks away.

Sheep stares at the mended fence.

She scurries outside and runs up to the fence.

She pushes on the boards. They won't budge an inch.

A fence without a hole ...

That's quite different from a fence you can walk through.

Sheep hobbles over to Goat. "Goat! We can't get out! The board has been hammered back on!"

Goat wakes up right away.

She looks at the fence with alarm. She runs up to it.

She pushes and she pulls.

The fence is nailed up tight.

Sheep goes to stand next to Goat. She gulps.

Goat gives Sheep a penetrating look.

"What do you think of our fence now, Sheep?" asks Goat.

"It's a little too shut now," says Sheep, feeling a little cramped.

"You didn't want to get out anyhow, did you?" says Goat.

"It's not that," squeaks Sheep. "But now we *can't* get out. That's the difference."

All at once Goat starts to run, way into the meadow.

Sheep totters along.

Goat stops at the corner. Between the clover and the thistles.

"We'll make a new hole!" cries Goat. "Look, Sheep, the wire from the fence is really loose here. We'll just push it aside. That will make a new hole."

Goat has already started in.

She pushes and she pulls. The wire hardly moves.

"Come help me!" cries Goat.

Sheep tugs on the wire, too.

It's not easy, but the opening in the wire gets bigger and bigger. Goat can already get through. It's still a bit too small for Sheep.

Goat pulls the wire even farther to the side.

"Try it now," she says.

Yes. Sheep fits.

She wiggles through the hole.

Goat steps through behind her.

They're both standing outside the meadow. On a soggy bit of earth.

"Where are we going to go?" asks Goat.

Their hooves sink all the way into the ground.

"Oh," says Sheep. "I don't really have to go anywhere right now. Maybe some other time ..."

Sheep pulls her hooves out of the mud.

She squeezes back through the bent wire.

Goat steps through the hole, too.

"I'm in the mood for a thistle," says Sheep.

And she bites into a great big thistle.

Goat starts in on the clover.

"The hole turned out well, didn't it, Sheep?" asks Goat with her mouth full.

"The hole turned out very well," answers Sheep.

It's quiet in the meadow now.

Dusk is falling.

The hole can no longer be seen.

But it's still there.